Whenever Monkeys Move Next Door

written and illustrated by

Deanna Plummer Wood

Perkins Crawford Literary Group
Huntsville, Alabama

Inquiries about this book should be addressed to:

Perkins Crawford Literary Group

www.perkinscrawford.com

Library of Congress Cataloging-in-Publication Data
Wood, Deanna Plummer

Whenever Monkeys Move Next Door / by Deanna Plummer Wood: Illustrations by Deanna Plummer Wood
Huntsville, AL Perkins Crawford Literary Group

p. cm.
Summary: Silliness abounds when a mischievous band of monkeys moves next door to a little boy and he attempts to round them up as they wreak havoc on the neighborhood.
ISBN 0-9762935-1-X

[1. Monkey-fiction. 2. Juvenile-fiction. 3. Stories in rhyme.] I. Wood, Deanna Plummer. II. Wood, Deanna Plummer, ill. III. Title

Printed and bound in the *United States of America*
By Xcel Printing Service, Huntsville, AL

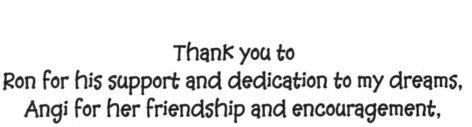

Thank you to
Ron for his support and dedication to my dreams,
Angi for her friendship and encouragement,

And the Father, Son, and Holy Spirit for all things.

For my little monkeys
Caroline and Kathleen
Matthew 19:14

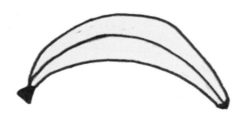

One lazy summer day
while hanging from
my climbing tree,
I was sad
because there was
no one to play with me.

My best friend
who lived next door
had just moved away.

Now I was all alone till someone
else moved in to stay.

Rumble, Rumble, Zoom!

A huge truck sped up the street,
and pulled into the driveway
of the house next door to me.

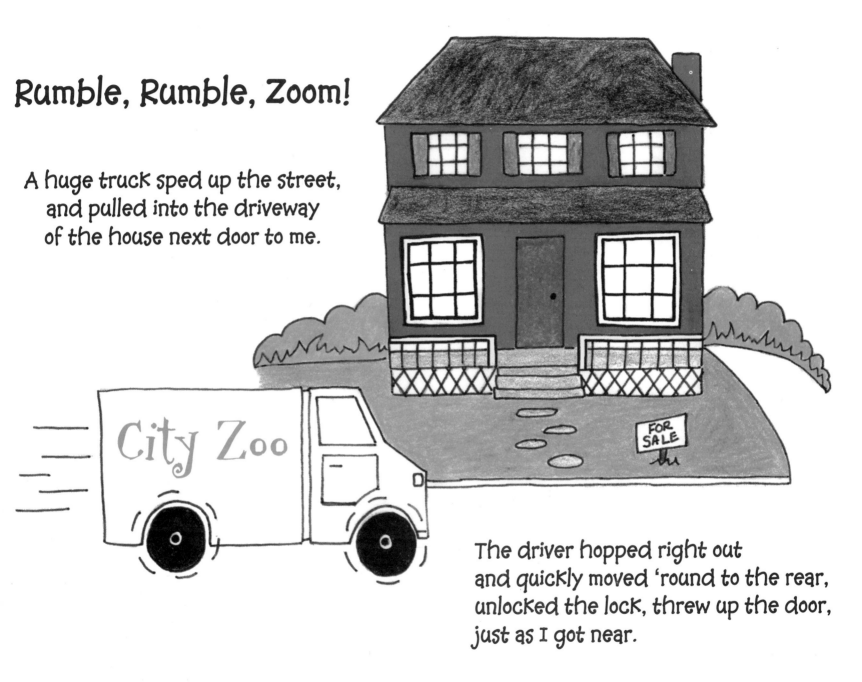

The driver hopped right out
and quickly moved 'round to the rear,
unlocked the lock, threw up the door,
just as I got near.

One, Two, Three, Four,
monkeys tumbled
out the door!

Four more followed,
that made eight.

Eight monkey neighbors,
oh, how great!

Nine, Ten, Eleven, Twelve, a dozen monkeys on the grass,
all hopping, flipping, spinning, from the first one to the last.

"Excuse me, sir," I asked him, "are these monkeys moving in?"
"Yes, son," he answered, smiling, "this is where they all will live!"

"And I wonder," he continued, "would you help me this one time?
It's not easy moving monkeys and they ought to be inside."

"Yes, of course!" I volunteered,
"Just tell me what to do."

"Oh, you'll do just fine," he said,
"as long as you remember to —"

RING, RING, RING

His cell phone interrupted us
and so he took the call.
His smile turned into a frown,
it wasn't good at all.

"I have to go," he said, "seems there's a problem at the zoo.
      I guess that means I'll have to leave the monkeys here with you!"

      "Wait, don't leave!" I shouted,
      as he drove his truck away,
      leaving me to move the monkeys
      that had just moved in that day.

I took a breath and turned around and was surprised to see,
twelve little pairs of monkey eyes all staring back at me.
A grin began to grow upon each little monkey face,
and grow and grow until each grin had run right out of space.

It was clear I was in trouble as each chattered to the other,
then suddenly dashed off in pairs - six teams of monkey brothers!

"Wait, don't run!" I ordered, "You're supposed to be inside!"
But monkeys don't take orders when they've made up their monkey minds.

I chased the first two down the street into Miss Yokel's yard,
but with four feet they were so fast, just keeping up was hard.

I found them in her flowers munching mums and gladiolas,
I chased them out with one loud shout, then saw two of the others!

They'd grabbed the cats of Mr. Blatt and Miss Belinda Blott,
and with those cats a'wailing tied their tails into a knot!
I started to rush over, but then saw to my surprise,
two monkeys in some garbage cans with trash up to their eyes!

Rotten old
banana peels
hung on
their ears
and
heads.
I dove for them,
but they
jumped out,
and I fell in
instead!

I climbed out covered in a sticky, green, disgusting slime,
then spotted two more monkeys
on my mommy's clean clothesline.
They swung round and round, looping high up in the air,
Knocked the clean clothes in the mud,
tried on my underwear!

I pulled them off,
then saw two topping Miss Gerbubbles' roof,
disappearing down her chimney with a big, black poof.
I ran inside to save her from their grimy, dirty paws,
and heard Miss Gerbubbles yell at them,
"Hey, you're not Santa Claus!"

She shooed us out her front door just in time for me to spot,
ten monkeys taking all the mail from everyone's mailbox.
They ripped and tore it up until confetti they had made,
and then those crazy monkeys had their own monkey parade!

Rumble, Rumble, Zoom!

The monkeys' truck raced up the street!
The driver got out at the curb, and chuckled at
the scene.

He said,
"I'm sorry for the trouble,
turns out the problem at the zoo,
was that the monkeys
belong there,
not living here
next door to you!"

"That's okay," I told him plainly,
"they're too much hard work anyway.
Now I know why Mommy's tired
after chasing me all day."

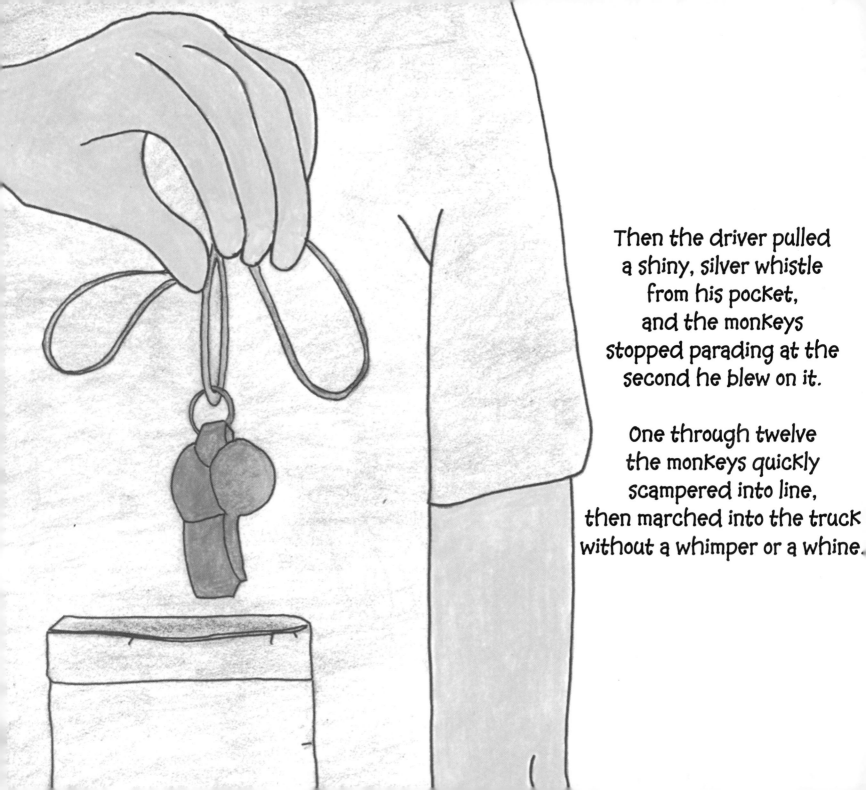

Then the driver pulled
a shiny, silver whistle
from his pocket,
and the monkeys
stopped parading at the
second he blew on it.

One through twelve
the monkeys quickly
scampered into line,
then marched into the truck
without a whimper or a whine.

He handed one banana to each behaving monkey,
    then closed the door and locked the lock
    and climbed into the front seat.

"That's the trick," the driver said,
    as he pulled away.
"Whistles and bananas get
    any monkey to obey!"

Now, you might think that having monkey neighbors would be fun,
But as for me, well, I was glad my monkey-ing was done.
I was covered in that green, gross slime and mail that they had shred,
it looked like a giant alien had sneezed over my head!
I had mud and dirt and soot from my left toe to my top hair,
(and don't tell, but I could smell trash still stuck in my underwear!)

But, now that you know my story,
you should know just what to do,
to make your life much easier
if you're ever in my shoes.

If you keep a whistle handy,
and twelve bananas (maybe more),
things won't be so crazy
whenever monkeys move next door!

The End

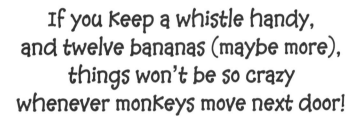